EASTER PARADE

EASTER PARADE

Mary Chalmers

Harper & Row, Publishers

Copyright © 1988 by Mary Chalmers
Printed in the U.S.A. All rights reserved.
1   2   3   4   5   6   7   8   9   10
First Edition

Library of Congress Cataloging-in-Publication Data
Chalmers, Mary, 1927–
Easter parade.

Summary: The Easter animals gather for a
springtime parade and everyone gets an Easter basket.
[1. Easter—Fiction.   2. Parades—Fiction.
3. Animals—Fiction]   I. Title.
PZ7.C354Eas 1988   [E]   87-45277
ISBN 0-06-021232-2
ISBN 0-06-021233-0 (lib. bdg.)

for Nina

Every spring there is an Easter Parade.
Easter Chickens come from the mountains.

Easter Rabbits come
from the fields and woods.

And Easter Ducks

come from the lake.

They all meet at Easter Farm

and load up their carts for the Easter Parade.

There is a basket for every little rabbit,

and every little possum,

for every little field mouse,

and every little kitten.

The Easter Parade has a basket

for every child.

At the very last house
they leave two big baskets.

But there is still one little basket left!

Who didn't get a basket?

The Easter animals look here,

and there,

and everywhere.

"You forgot the ladybug!" calls the bluebird.

Now, when the ladybug wakes up,
she will have her Easter basket, too.

The parade rolls back to Easter Farm,

and the Easter animals say their good-byes.

Then the Easter Ducks go back
to their lake.

The Easter Rabbits go back
to their fields and woods.

And the Easter Chickens go back

to their mountains...

until next spring.